WICKED SUMMER KNIGHT

KNIGHT'S RIDGE EMPIRE: PREQUEL

TRACY LORRAINE

NOTE

Wicked Summer Knight is set in London and everyone aside from Stella speaks in British English. This may mean that spellings look incorrect compared to what you're used to.

WICKED SUMMER KNIGHT

She's in the wrong place at the right time...

Gunshots echo, reverberating through me, allowing me to feel something... anything other than the pain that consumes me.

That should be a warning to stay away, but for some reason, she comes closer. Intruding on my silence. Sharing my darkness.

Close enough for me to see the look in her eyes. It's not fear, but desire that darkens her eyes in the moonlight.

She should run. Run far away from me, but she

never does. She comes close enough to touch, tempting the devil inside that wants to cause devastation for the loss I've suffered.

I take what I need before I discover the truth. The gorgeous girl in the shadows that tastes like sin, isn't an angel coming to light my way.

She's one of us.
One I never should have touched.
And she has no idea.

She could be my destruction...

STELLA

With a loud groan, I fall back onto my bed. It feels like the walls are closing in on me.

Twisting my head to the side, I stare out of the window at the quickly descending sun. The summer in London has been incredible— nothing like I was expecting when I told people where I was moving this time.

To everyone on the other side of the pond, all it does in England is rain.

Well, the sunburn on my shoulders is proof that that isn't actually the case.

We've been here almost two months, and other than sitting in the yard, I can count on one hand the number of times I've actually left the house.

I mean, I'm not entirely sure where I'd go if I did, but I'm starting to lose my mind. Like I'm forgetting who I really am.

Dad knows he can trust me, so the fact that he's requested that I don't go anywhere without him tells me that he's deadly serious. So as much as it's killed me, I've stayed put while he's disappeared off to wherever he goes.

I shouldn't complain; of all the houses we've lived in over the years, this is by far one of the nicest. I don't even want to think about just how much it must cost. The only thing I'm missing is space, but then I guess this is London, not Montana.

I blow out a breath as I stare at the burning orange sun that's descending behind the trees at the end of our yard.

My fingers twist in the sheets beneath me with my need to get out. With my need to move... and not just in the basement gym. I need to reconnect with the person I am outside of these four walls that are beginning to feel like a prison.

"Fuck it," I mutter, jumping up and pulling my closet door open.

I find a pair of sneakers and drag them on my feet before heading out of my room.

The house, as always, is in silence. I've got the entire second floor to myself. It's totally over the top and unnecessary, but Dad has always been the same. All the houses we've lived in have been way too big for the two of us and the couple of staff he employs.

I come to a stop at the kitchen door when I hear Angie, our housekeeper, crashing around, probably tidying up from dinner.

I don't want to sneak out. I don't want to be that person. But equally, I don't want her to call Dad the second I turn my back and to have to deal with him knowing that I ignored his wishes.

"Evenin' Mrs. A," I announce as I march into the room.

"Is there something you need, honey?" Angie asks softly, standing from where she was loading the dishwasher.

"No, thank you." Although it soon becomes clear that's a lie when I stop in front of one specific cupboard and pull it open.

"Estella," she growls when my hand reappears with my fingers wrapped around the neck of a bottle of vodka, although I don't miss the glint in her eye.

"What?" I ask with a smile, hopping up onto the cool marble counter. "It's not like I've got anything else to do around here." Her lips part to respond, but no words leave her mouth as I swallow my first shot. It burns all the way down my throat, just like I needed. She knows I'm right. "Any word on when Dad will be home?"

"He said he'd be late."

"Great." I roll my eyes and take another shot. "At least here this is almost legal, right?"

"Please don't drink all of that tonight," she pleads, eyeing the bottle.

"Oh come on, I know you were a wild child back in the day, Mrs. A."

"Uh—"

"I'm going to bed with my friend here." I wiggle the bottle at her cutting off her lie with a sassy smile on my lips.

"Stella, I—"

"Have a good evening, Angie. Night." I wave

her off as I slip out of the room and move toward the stairs in case she's watching.

Glancing behind me, I double back and head for the rear of the house in the hope that I can slip out without security noticing.

The sticky summer air hits me the second I step out of the sliding doors and into the backyard. The sun might have gone down, but it's still hot as hell, and my hair is sticking to the back of my neck long before I escape through the back gate and out onto the street.

I smile to myself, feeling like a rebel. It's nothing really, just going out for a walk, but my dad never jokes about things, especially when it comes to my safety, so I know he's serious about me staying inside. I just wish he'd tell me the reason, so at least I could understand instead of remaining hidden from some unknown threat.

I take off down the peaceful, treelined street.

I have no destination in mind. I've only ever come down here in Dad's car, seeing as mine hasn't arrived yet.

Aside from the friends I left behind in

America, my car is one of the only other things I miss. My matte black Porsche 911. It was my baby, and I can't wait for my new one to be delivered. Hopefully, that will grant me a little bit of an escape. No one can get to me while I'm driving.

The honking of car horns sounds out in the distance, a reminder that the hustle and bustle of the city is only meters away. It's easy to forget while I'm hiding in the house that we're not in the middle of nowhere here.

The first week we arrived, Dad took me to see all the sights London had to offer, and he showed me some of the places he used to spend time at when he was a kid.

I'm desperate to learn more, to meet some of his old friends. I would say family, but I already know I don't have any.

I blow out a breath as I continue walking, tipping the bottle to my lips once more and allowing the slight buzz from the vodka to numb me. The sun has long set now, and the only lights guiding my way are the streetlights above my head as I turn down street after street, gazing into the windows of the houses that have their lights on and curtains open, trying to get a sense of the people inside.

I have no idea where I'm going, but for the first time since moving here, I feel free.

I should enjoy having absolutely nothing to do, being able to breathe for a few weeks before I'm thrust into the middle of yet another school to start over at yet again, but I'm not. I think I'd rather be enduring all the unknowns and stresses of a new school. I've almost lost count of the number I've attended over the years thanks to Dad moving us all over the country. He's assured me that this is it. That we're staying here and that I might actually be able to graduate. Although, moving here came at a price. I'm going back a year. If I were still in America and attending Rosewood High, I'd have already started my senior year along with my friends, but as it is, I'm about to embark on my first year in a British sixth form instead.

I don't want nor need another year before I can finally make my own decisions about life and where I might want to go to college or university, but it seems I have little choice in the matter.

Part of me wanted to stay in America and

let Dad move back here alone. I'm pretty sure if I'd asked and pleaded a good enough case he'd have allowed it... I'm almost eighteen, after all, and he knows I'm sensible enough not to screw shit up, but while most of my life has been a clusterfuck of moving house, state and country, he has been my one constant. Yes, he's always worked more than he's been at home, and at times it's felt like I've been brought up by the housekeeper or our security, but he's always been there, even if it's been at the end of the phone.

It's been me and Dad against the world, and the thought of watching him get on an airplane and fly across the world without me wrecks me even now that I'm here with him.

He's the only person I have, my only family, and despite us sometimes having our differences, he's my best friend.

I continue walking as the air around me finally begins to cool and the moon rises in the sky. My cell burns in my skirt pocket, but I don't pull it out to look at the time. I don't want to know if my absence has been noticed yet, and I certainly don't want to have to deal with Dad's disappointment if he knows that I've ignored him and walked straight out the front gate alone.

My steps slowdown as a familiar pop echoes through the silence around me. Glancing to my right, I find that I'm beside a graveyard.

The sensible thing to do would be to turn around and head home in the hope that I can sneak back inside unnoticed and silently revel in the fact that I managed to escape and just breathe for a few hours, but that isn't what I do.

When I take another step, it's not toward home but into the darkness of the graveyard and toward the sound that stupidly speaks to my soul.

There are soft lights illuminating the church behind as well as lining the perimeter wall. They're enough to allow me to see the path that cuts through the grass and leads me into the darkness.

The pop sounds out again, but it's louder this time, telling me that my instincts were right.

But why would someone be firing off rounds in a graveyard in the middle of the night?

Dad has always said that my curiosity will get me killed, and it seems he might be right. But even knowing that I'm walking toward someone dangerous, my steps don't falter as my sneakers connect with the grass.

I come to a stop by an old oak tree and cast my eyes around the dark, creepy space until my eyes land on a figure sitting with his back resting against a headstone.

The moonlight casts a silvery light over his angular face. Hiding in the shadows, I take in his strong, square jaw and perfectly straight nose. He's dressed head to toe in black, his body blending into the darkness surrounding him. The only thing that really stands out is his outstretched arm and the metal in his hand glinting in the silver moonlight. My eyes focus on it, and I'm unable to look away as he fires it once more, the ting that quickly follows telling me that he hits whatever target he was aiming at.

After long seconds, I manage to rip my eyes away and focus on his face once more. I can't see much, but what I can draws me to him in a way I can't explain.

He's a stranger in a graveyard with a gun. I

should be running in the opposite direction, but something forces me to do the opposite.

I step out from behind the tree and move toward him, my heart thundering in my chest when a twig snaps under my foot and both his eyes and gun turn to me.

2

SEBASTIAN

I narrow my eyes, focusing on my target —the next can in line along the dry stone wall at the very back of the graveyard.

No one ever comes back here at this time of night. I should know; I've spent enough time here over the past few years.

I squeeze my finger, and the gun in my hand ricochets as it shoots, the can I was focusing on crumpling and toppling over the back of the wall with all the others.

The scent of the gunpowder from the shot settles something inside me and my muscles relax for a beat, but it's not enough. It's never enough to calm the beast that lives inside me.

Blowing out a long breath, I curl my free hand into a fist, allowing my short nails to dig into my palm, cutting into the skin and giving me the pain I so desperately crave.

Lowering the gun, I stare down at the black metal casing of my pistol, of my fingers wrapped tightly around the handle. It would be so easy to put an end to it all. No one would even find me here for a few days, I'm sure. Whether it's day or night, this graveyard is always deserted.

Sadness and pain tug at my heart that the others who have ended up here have been forgotten by those they loved, that the ones they've left behind can't even find the time to come here and bring some flowers, to show that despite the fact they're no longer here, that they're still a part of their lives.

No matter how many times I've had the same thought, about putting an end to the pain and joining those who left me, I know I could never do it.

My need for vengeance burns too hot. It eats at me, consuming a little bit more of me every single day, extinguishing my light one piece at a time.

With a sigh, I raise my arm once more, aiming for the next can I've lined up.

With precision that only comes with years of practice and training, I shoot off one after another as the gunshots echo in the silence around me.

My chest heaves as I line up my next shot. My finger twitches and my body tenses, but before I can pull the trigger, something cracks to my right and I immediately twist around, aiming my gun at whoever is stupid enough to approach me.

The only people who might know where to find me know better than to interrupt.

My eyes blur a little as I try to focus on the figure in the shadows instead of the cans that were illuminated by the moon.

"What do you want?" I bark, irritated that the person won't show themselves yet were brave enough to stand there in the first place.

The silence stretches out between us before they step forward and into the light.

My breath catches in my throat when I realise the person who's interrupted me isn't a guy like I first thought, but a young woman. A really fucking hot young woman.

But the sight of her curves, of her light hair hanging around her shoulders, doesn't make me lower my gun. And she doesn't look the least bit fazed that I'm pointing it right between her brows.

"What do you want?" I ask again, a frown forming as I try to figure out why she didn't run the moment she realised I have a gun.

She takes another step forward and my brows shoot up in shock.

"You do realise I've got a gun pointed at your head, right?"

"You won't shoot me," she says with a confidence she really shouldn't feel. But it's not just that which surprises me. She's American. Her light but slightly raspy accented voice flows through me, making my hairs stand on end.

Who is this girl? And why do I want her to keep talking?

"You don't know me. You have no idea what I'm capable of."

"That may be true. But you won't shoot me."

Once she's close enough, she lifts her hand and wraps her fingers around the barrel of my gun, showing just how unconcerned she really is, before putting a little pressure on it until my arm drops.

If she were anyone else, I wouldn't allow it, but I'm too flabbergasted to fight her.

"You need to leave," I tell her.

"You're probably right. But I'm here now."

She steps right up to me, our bodies only an inch from each other's.

"How about a game?" she suggests.

"Uh..."

"I take out your last few cans, and I get to do what I want. I miss even one, and I'll leave you to your pity party."

"N-no, this isn't—"

She shakes her head, looking up at me with a small smile playing on her lips.

Fuck, she's beautiful. Up close I can see that her hair is blonde, but not just blonde. It's almost white. She's got the longest eyelashes I think I've ever seen, her skin looks flawless, and her lips... fuck. I bite down on my bottom one as I imagine what they might taste like.

"So, what do you say?" she asks innocently, although the glint in her eye and the fact that she's standing before me without any hesitation tells me that she's anything but. An innocent girl would have run. Hell, an innocent girl wouldn't be walking through a deserted graveyard in the middle of the night.

I lower my eyes to her body. She's wearing a tank and a short skirt. Although it's been a scorching hot day, I'm surprised she's not feeling a little cool right now, but she doesn't look bothered in the slightest.

"Okay," I agree, finding her light eyes once more. I can't make out the colour, but I know I could easily get lost in them. I drop my eyes once more and take a step closer. "I think I've already changed my mind about what I want when I win."

"It would be wise if you didn't underestimate me." She closes the last bit of space between us, her breasts brushing my chest, making my breath catch in my throat.

Girl's got balls, I'll give her that.

Her fingers skim down my arm before sliding against mine to take my gun.

Our eyes remain locked, something I've never experienced before crackling between us as the heat of her body burns through my hoodie, making my temperature soar.

"Get ready to lose."

She slips around me, her feet crunching the fallen leaves underfoot.

By the time I turn around, she's sitting exactly where I was earlier with her back against the headstone and her eyes focused on the cans that are remaining on the wall.

With her long bare legs stretched out in front of her, she lifts her arm and aims the gun at my remaining targets.

I'm instantly hard.

Reaching up, I run my fingers through my hair, knocking my hood off my head and wrapping my hand around the back of my neck, wondering if this is even real.

Did the joint I smoked a few hours ago have some weird shit in it? Am I hallucinating? Because this girl can't be fucking real. She fucking can't be.

I'm so lost in my own thoughts that when she fires, my entire body jolts, my heart jumping into my throat as I rip my eyes from her to see if she actually hit anything.

Before I can find the missing can, she fires again, and I just about catch that one falling over the back of the wall.

Holy shit.

She fires again and again, taking out each can like a pro.

By the time I turn my stare back to her, she's up from the cool ground and walking toward me, my pistol hanging from her fingers.

No words are said, but I can read the I *told you so* on the tip of her tongue.

"You're going to need to do more than that to impress me, sweetheart." My eyes leisurely trail down her body, lingering on her full breasts straining against her tank.

"I don't go out of my way to impress anyone, *sweetheart.*"

My cock jumps at her confidence, at her gives-zero-fucks attitude. It's so refreshing and nothing like the girls I'm used to spending time with. The girls at school are all for impressing us, desperate to be exactly what we need. They might be hot, sure. But it's only skin deep.

This girl is... fuck if I know. But hell if I don't want her.

"Fair enough," I mutter, not hiding the fact that I'm stripping her naked with my eyes.

Dragging my hair back from my eyes once more, I finally look up into her eyes, which are significantly darker than before.

"Where did you learn to shoot like that?" I ask, too curious about her skills to keep the question to myself.

"I could ask you the same thing."

I nod at her. Even if she were to ask, she'd never get the truth out of me.

"You should be scared of me," I warn, dropping the tone of my voice to one that usually scares off guys who are much more dangerous than her at... what? Five foot four? With curves for miles.

She throws her head back and laughs, causing my fists to clench at my sides.

"Of you? I've put men twice your size on the floor with almost zero effort. I—"

3

STELLA

ll the air rushes from my lungs as my back slams against the oak tree I was hiding behind not so long ago. Whatever I was about to say is forgotten as his burning hot fingers wrap around my throat, squeezing hard enough that it makes white lights flicker across my vision.

My heart thunders in my chest as his dark eyes bore down into mine and his hot breath flows over my face, proving that he's as worked up as I am right now.

Only, I haven't worked him out yet. And while I'm excited by this unexpected interaction, I have no idea if he's downright furious that I've interrupted him and his little makeshift target practice session, or if he wants me as much as I do him.

We might be surrounded by darkness, but I'm pretty sure that we could be bathed in sunlight and his face would be just as unreadable as it is now. I like to think I'm good at reading people, but it's like he's wearing a mask.

His jaw ticks, his lips are pulled into a thin line, and his eyes are dangerously dark—with desire or anger, I have no idea, but fuck if they don't call to me, make me want to dive headfirst in the darkness of them and the aura that surrounds him.

I have no idea who he is or why he's here alone in the middle of the night, but I don't doubt the fact that I probably should be scared of him. I'm sure most other people would be.

But I'm not most people.

I've spent my life training to deal with men just like him, and what I said earlier was no lie. I've taken down more than I can count, and despite the fact that he thinks he's got the upper hand right now with his fingertips digging into the flesh of my throat, he doesn't realize it's exactly where I want to be. And if I wanted out, I could have him cowering away from me in seconds.

He's totally underestimating me, and I'll allow it to continue. For now.

His wicked eyes bounce between mine as he tries to read me, to understand me. Good fucking luck, asshole. No one else has managed to do it, so I really doubt he's going to be the one to get under my skin.

And to prove my point, instead of panicking or reacting in a 'normal' way, all I do is smile at him.

"You seem to be forgetting something," I say lightly.

"Oh yeah? What's that, sweetheart?" His deep voice rolls through me, making my lower stomach clench with desire and sending a wave of heat between my thighs.

"I've still got this." Lifting my hand, I trace the barrel of his gun up the side of his face until I rest it against his temple.

He swallows, the skin of his neck rippling with the move, but his eyes flash with danger. A danger that has butterflies erupting in my belly. Excitement surges through my veins as his scent fills my nose and his closeness makes my skin tingle.

I know what everyone thinks of me at first impression. They think I'm some young, weak girl. But they couldn't be further from the truth. One of my favorite hobbies is proving just how wrong they are, and I have a suspicion that doing it right now is going to be one of the sweetest.

This guy thinks he's dangerous. To be fair, he probably is; it's the reason I'm drawn to him. If I've learned anything about myself in my almost eighteen years, it's that my ultimate weakness is the baddest of the bad boys.

His lips curl into a cocky smirk that makes me want to melt, his eyes continuing to hold mine, his silent warning coming through to me loud and clear. It's just a shame I'm going to ignore it.

"If you think that's going to scare me then you need to reconsider, sweetheart."

I have no idea if he's aware of the fact that I've just shot his last bullet or not, but I'm more than happy to pretend, because I can't deny that this little bit of gunplay has me desperate for more.

Who knew when I slipped out of my house tonight for some space that I'd stumble across exactly what I really needed?

Him.

It might have only been weeks since we arrived here, but hell if I'm not missing people. Talking to my friends on video chat is great and all, but it's no match for being face to face —skin to skin—with someone.

"I'm not trying to do anything," I lie. "I won, so it's only right that I'm the one in control right now."

"So you did," he murmurs, his deep voice reverberating through me. "What do you want as your reward? Freedom?"

"Freedom?" I ask, my brows pulling together.

"Any sensible person would turn around and walk away from me as fast as they appeared."

"In case you hadn't noticed, I'm not exactly normal," I confess.

The warm fingers of his free hand wrap around mine on his gun, and when he pulls it away from his head, I allow it. Only because

I'm assuming what's coming next, and I crave it like a junkie needs his next hit.

I flinch when the cool metal of his gun connects with my cheek, but it's not with fear. It's with desire.

My lips part, and a low groan rumbles up my throat.

"Who are you?" he asks, his nose mimicking the movement of the gun on the other side of my face. Only he's soft and warm compared to the cold hardness of the metal.

"Either your worst nightmare or your perfect woman."

He pauses, his entire body going rigid, before the most incredible sound falls from him. He laughs.

"I think you might be right there, sweetheart."

"You might need to reconsider that little nickname, stranger. I'm not sweet, and I'm not entirely sure I have a heart either."

"So you're not an angel who's fallen straight from heaven for me then?" he whispers in my ear, his lips brushing the shell and sending a shiver down my spine.

"I'm pretty sure I came straight from hell."

He pulls back and his eyes flash with heat before they drop to my lips. I suck my bottom one into my mouth as I imagine once more how his might feel moving against mine, just how hard he's likely to bite.

The gun that's still resting on my cheek begins to descend, running over my jaw and down my neck. His eyes follow its movement all the way down my chest until he begins to drag the fabric down to expose my bra.

I swallow as desire threatens to consume me, my nipples pressing almost painfully against the padding of my bra. He hasn't even touched me and I'm damn near panting for him.

"So what's it going to be, Hellion?"

A smile curls at my lips at my new name.

My chest heaves, and when he feels me swallow against his hold, his eyes lift to mine once more.

Something crackles loudly, drawing me to him even more than I was when I saw him sitting there with his gun in his hand.

Unable to resist his full lips, I lean forward, but before I manage to make contact, his hold on my throat tightens and I have no choice but to freeze.

"Make no mistake, Hellion. You might have won, but you'll never be in charge."

I hold his eyes, accepting his challenge.

He must be able to read my thoughts, because a smirk curls at his lips before he closes the space he kept between us.

"You're going to regret this," he warns, lips only a breath from mine.

"I very much doubt it. Do your worst, hotshot."

His lips slam down on mine with a force that shocks me in the best of ways. Our teeth clash and our tongues duel for dominance, but I think we both know who's going to win the fight—mainly because I want him to.

His fingers flex against my throat in warning, but it only serves to make me burn hotter for him.

The hardness of his gun drops from my chest, and a second later, a low thud fills my ears as he presses the length of his body against mine. His hand lands on my waist, his skin scorching me through my tank.

Dropping lower, he finds the bare skin of

my thigh and hooks my leg around his waist, opening me up to him and ensuring that I can't miss just how into this he is right now. His hard length presses exactly where I need him, causing a low groan to rumble up my throat.

Ripping his lips from mine, he releases my throat and trails light kisses down over my sensitive skin.

"I have no idea who you are, or where you came from, but you're mine now."

"Oh God," I cry when his lips part and he sucks on my skin until it begins to burn.

My fingers twist in his hoodie, but I have no idea if it's to push him away because it hurts or to drag him closer and force him to continue.

I'm fed up of living in the confines of my house, hidden away like some princess in a castle.

I need to remember who I am. I need this excitement, this pain, this high.

He releases me with a pop, but he doesn't let up, instead sucking and biting all the way down over my collarbone and to the edge of my tank.

My breasts are heavy with my need for him to touch me, and I sigh in relief when he tugs the straps of both my top and bra over my shoulder and pulls down until he exposes me.

"Maybe a part of you did fall from heaven, Hellion."

"No, I—" My response dies on my lips when he sucks one hard peak into his mouth, his tongue swirling around the sensitive skin before his teeth sink in.

"Fuck, fuck." My fingers thread into his hair, twisting painfully as he continues his assault.

I lose myself to the sensations as he switches from one side to the other to continue driving me crazy.

My panties are soaked, my clit pulsating with my need to be touched, my need to fall over the edge at his command.

I get to the point where I almost think he'll manage it from just this alone, when he abruptly pulls back and stands before me.

"W-wha—"

"Get on our knees." His words are like fuel to my already out of control fire as his dark, wicked eyes bore into mine. I don't need to look at the rest of his expression to know that he's deadly serious. I'm not sure whether this guy ever actually jokes about anything.

His hand grips my bare shoulder and he pushes forcefully until my knees buckle beneath me—not that I really need the encouragement. My mouth is already watering for what's about to happen.

Excitement surges through me, for in that moment I finally take total control over this situation without even really having to do anything.

The second I'm on my haunches before him, I reach out, lifting his hoodie and finding the button of his waistband.

I waste no time in popping it open and wrapping my fingers around the fabric of both his pants and boxers and pulling them down.

My eyes have long adjusted to the darkness, and although I can't make everything out, I know instantly that he has a very good reason for being a cocky asshole, because he's not just packing in the gun department.

Lifting my hand, I wrap my fingers around his length and lean forward, licking at the tip that's glistening in the moonlight. His taste explodes on my tongue, making my mouth water even more to feel him hitting the back of my throat.

His hips thrust forward at my contact, trying to take more. He'll wait. He might not understand that he's lost his control right now, but he'll learn.

Licking the tip of him like a popsicle, I look up.

My breath catches at the menacing expression on his face.

"Hellion," he growls, clearly unimpressed with my teasing.

I continue to hold his eyes as I move forward, allowing the head of his cock to pass my lips.

"Fuck," he barks as I continue sucking him deeper. His fingers twist in my hair until it burns and causes heat and need to explode within me. But he doesn't take control of my movements like I was expecting him to. Not yet, at least.

I take him back as far as I can before pulling off and teasing the underside of his cock with my tongue as I release him.

"You're right. You're certainly no angel," he growls as I take him again, deeper this time, making his length jerk in my mouth.

His hold on me tightens as his hips begin to

move, keeping himself deep in my throat. Saliva spills from the side of my mouth as my eyes burn and water with my need for air.

"Yesss," he hisses as his thrusts get more demanding.

His cock swells even more in my mouth, and I prepare myself for him to come down my throat.

But as I expect it to happen, his fingers tighten even more in my hair until I swear he's about to rip it clean from my head, and I'm pulled off his cock and dragged to my feet.

I've barely found my balance, my head still spinning from my lack of air when his lips slam down on mine, his tongue plunging in my mouth as his hands skim up the outside of my thighs, pushing my skirt up around my waist.

His fingers wrap around the sides of my panties and I bite down on his tongue the second the sound of ripping fabric hits my ears before the cool night air breezes past my most intimate place.

Still kissing me as if he needs my air to live, he kicks my legs apart and cups my pussy with his hot fingers.

"Mine," he growls into our kiss before

moaning in delight when he feels the surge of wetness his declaration causes.

I have no idea who this guy is, if he's as dangerous as he makes himself out to be, but fuck if I care right now. With his gun at our feet and his hands on my body, I feel more like myself than I have since I got on that plane at Orlando International, leaving my previous life behind. But in this moment, I don't care, because he's giving me back a part of myself that I thought I'd left in America.

I've been a boring shell of myself since getting here, putting on a show for Dad because I know this is where he wants to be, even if he won't confide in me why he chose now to come back. But right now, I can feel the old Stella emerging to the surface once more, and fuck, it feels so fucking good.

His finger slides through my folds and a shudder rips through my body when it finds my clit and applies the perfect amount of pressure as he begins circling it.

"Fuck me," I moan into his mouth.

"Jesus, Hellion. I must have done something fucking right in my life to deserve this."

He pushes his fingers back, finding my entrance. He circles a couple of times, stretching me open and driving me crazy with my need to feel him inside me. When he does put a digit inside me, a loud growl of approval rips from my throat. My head falls back, colliding with the tree behind me, but I barely feel it as he bends his fingers just so.

"So wet for me, Hellion. And so tight."

"Please." The word falls from my lips as a whimper. I sound needy and desperate, but fuck if I care right now.

With his hand around the back of my neck, he drags me back to his lips as his fingers leave me.

I want to cry out at the loss, but I manage to contain it.

I lose myself in his kiss, running my hands up his solid chest and draping my arms over his shoulders as he gets himself ready.

His lips leave mine so he can rip the condom packet open, and, in record time, he's sheathed and lifting me from the ground.

My legs automatically wrap around his waist, my exposed back scratching against the tree trunk behind me.

"If you were expecting someone soft and gentle, then you really approached the wrong guy tonight."

"What part of our interaction makes you think that's what I want?" I say, staring dead into his eyes as he teases me with the head of his cock. "Fuck. Me. Stranger," I demand, and it seems he's unable to do anything but comply. "Fuuuuuck," I moan when he stretches me so wide it burns.

It's been way too long since I was with anyone, but I knew that before I stumbled across this guy. I also knew he was exactly what I needed the second I looked into his wicked eyes.

4

SEBASTIAN

oly fuck.

My eyes squeeze closed as her heat surrounds me and her velvet walls suck me deeper.

I've had plenty of pussy in the past few years, but fuck if she isn't better than all of them.

I'm not sure if it's because of today's date and what it signifies, or if she's a stranger that I most likely will never see again after tonight, or the fact that it's so dark out that we can only make out the basic details of each other, but something about this encounter is more powerful, more electric than any I've experienced before.

It's probably because she threatened you with your own gun, a little voice says in the back of my head.

She's got the balls of one of the guys, and fuck if that's not a massive fucking turn-on.

My fingertips dig into the skin of her thighs, and I push deeper inside her.

Fuck, I needed this tonight.

I needed to get out of my own head, to push my need for vengeance, for blood, aside and focus on something else.

She might say she wasn't an angel sent from heaven, but hell if it doesn't feel exactly like she was sent here for me tonight.

If she hadn't stumbled upon me, who knows how tonight would have ended.

Releasing one of her legs, I thread my fingers back into her hair and drag her head back, exposing her neck to me.

I'm sure it's already littered with hickeys, but I can't stop myself from giving her more.

I might not ever see her again, let alone recognise her, but at least this way, if we do happen to stumble upon each other once more, like fate or some shit, then at least I'll know for sure it's her if she's wearing my mark.

I pull almost all the way out of her as I suck on her neck before surging back into her, my teeth grinding as her muscles clamp down on me so tight I could come on the spot if I'm not careful.

I'm not that kind of a man. I might be a cunt in many, many ways, but she deserves to at least come first tonight.

"Oh G-God," she moans as I circle my hips before I begin to up my tempo with my need to let go.

Tonight is already the worst kind of torture; I don't need to add more to it.

I kiss around her neck, dragging the skin into my mouth and grazing it with my teeth. Every time it hurts, her pussy contracts, forcing me closer to the end.

Finally, when I'm almost at the point of no return, I release her hair in favour of her clit and pinch down hard as I thrust inside her, making her slide up the tree.

"Yes," she cries. "Fucking yes."

Her fingers tighten in the hair at the nape of my neck as she tries to move against me to find her release.

"Come, Hellion. Come on my fucking cock,"

I growl into her ear seconds before she shatters, crying out so loudly into the silence surrounding us that a couple of birds take flight from the tree above us.

Sinking my teeth into the soft skin of her neck until the taste of copper fills my mouth, I allow her to drag me over the edge with her and groan out my release as my cock jerks inside her.

I just fucking wish I were bare and that she was forced to feel me inside her for hours to come.

That thought hits me out of nowhere and makes my breathing even more ragged than it already is. I never take girls bare. Ever. I've never even thought about it before. The risk of what could happen always makes it not worth it. But suddenly, all I can think about is her cunt with my cum dripping out of it.

Fuck.

With my face still in the crook of her neck, we both fight to control our racing hearts before she attempts to unwrap herself from me.

"What are you doing?" I ask, the panic in my tone a little too obvious for my liking.

"We both got what we wanted," she says coldly.

"Nah, Hellion," I say, allowing her to get to her feet. "I'm not fucking done with you yet."

A yelp of shock passes her lips as I spin her around and pin her against the tree. Once I've pulled the condom off, I press the length of my body against hers, my cock lining up with her round arse, making it begin to swell once more. That tells me everything I need to know. That was not enough. Not by a long shot.

"You'll leave when I tell you to. You got that?"

"Y-yes," she stutters, but I swear to God I hear a smile in it.

"Good girl. Now hold the tree and stick your arse out. I need to taste this pussy that belongs to me."

I feel the violent shudder that rips through her at my words before I pull back and allow her to move into position.

Dropping to my knees behind her, I wrap my hands around her thighs and dive for her slick pussy. The taste of latex from the condom soon fades, leaving me with only her sweetness to feast on.

I eat her like a starved man until her legs tremble and she's crying out, begging for me to let her fall, but as much as I might want her to shatter on my face, that's not how this ends. The only time she's coming tonight is with my cock buried balls deep inside her.

Pulling back from her, I wipe the back of my hand across my mouth and stand.

Wrapping the length of her hair around my fist, I pull her back flush to my chest.

"Tell me you're clean and on birth control."

"Y-yes. I am."

"Good."

Pushing her back down, I take my hard length in my hand and almost immediately thrust straight inside her.

Our grunts and moans of pleasure echo around us as I drive into her with abandon. She holds herself up against the tree, but as she gets closer to her release, her arms begin to give out. My grip on her hips tightens to hold her upright as sweat starts to run down my back with my exertion.

"Come, Hellion."

I reach around her and pinch her clit once more and she detonates. The second her muscles clamp down around me, I fall with her, spurting hot jets of cum inside her and settling that incessant need I had to leave my mark in this woman.

"Fuck," I pant, reluctantly pulling out of her and this time tucking myself away, knowing that our time has come to an end.

As much as I might want to keep her, I know I can't.

I need to take this for what it is: a little bit of luck on the worst day of the year.

I'm fucking grateful for whoever sent her my way tonight, but I'm not going to take the piss. Good shit like this doesn't usually happen to guys like me, so I need to take what I can.

I take a few steps back, running my hand through my hair and pushing it from my brow as she stands up straight and rights her skirt to cover herself up. It's a damn fucking shame, because she's got a fine arse.

She keeps her back to me as she smooths her hair down, and, I assume, as she cleans up her face.

My heart aches as I stare at her, knowing that I'm about to be forced to watch her walk away when a huge part of me wants to demand she stays.

Finally, she looks over her shoulder at me. I can tell by the expression on her face that she knows this is over too.

It's the right thing to do, to let her walk away. No one deserves to be a part of my bullshit life. I don't want to even be a part of it, but I have little choice.

My fate was sealed the day I was born due to the blood that runs through my veins.

She can have a better life, one I'm sure she deserves despite the fact that she thinks she's fallen straight from hell.

"Well, thanks, I guess. I really needed that."

I'd laugh if it weren't for the serious look on her face.

Her eyes flick down to my gun that's still sitting in the grass at her feet.

Shooting her foot out, she kicks it over to me and I bend down to pick it up.

I'm still looking at it when I hear the shuffle of her feet as she begins to walk away.

She's almost out of sight when my lips part and I call her back without realising what I'm actually doing.

"W-wait."

She pauses, but she doesn't look back.

"What's your name?" I ask, needing to know just something about her after everything she's given me tonight.

She freezes for a few seconds, long enough that I don't think she's going to respond.

But then she turns.

Her eyes hold mine, that familiar chemistry crackling between us as if I've not just had her twice in the space of thirty minutes.

Her lips open and then close again as if she's battling with herself as to whether she should tell me or not.

I'm about to tell her to forget it, to just leave it as a mystery that we can both fondly remember, when she finally speaks.

"It's Stella." My heart begins to race.

No. There's no fucking way.

"Stella Doukas."

All the air in my lungs rushes out, my chest aching with my need to breathe, but I can't.

My fists curl at my sides as anger like I've only ever experienced a couple of times in my life surges through me.

I fight like hell to keep my expression

neutral so she'll turn and leave once more, because if she reads anything on my face right now then there's a very good chance she won't leave this graveyard alive.

"And you?"

I shake my head, unable to even recall my own name right now as I stare into her traitorous eyes.

"Your worst fucking nightmare, Hellion."

5

STELLA

I stand in front of my full-length mirror and screw up my nose at the reflection staring back at me.

Another new day, another new school.

I'm already well prepared for the assessing looks from the bitchy girls as they try to work out if I'm going to come in and steal the boys they want, to roll off my back. So does their judgment. I don't give a shit what they think of me, if my hair is styled in a way they accept, or if my makeup is on point. I'm sure the second they hear me speak they'll realize that I don't belong here and turn their vapid comments toward me.

Whatever.

I roll my eyes to myself.

I've never needed validation from anyone else, and I certainly don't need it from the girls who think they run Knight's Ridge College.

I run my fingers down the soft fabric of the tie around my neck.

I'm not used to this. None of the schools I attended in America had a uniform. It feels weird, knowing that I'm going to be dressed exactly the same as everyone else there. I can't deny that I can see the obvious benefits. Thanks to Dad's business, we've always had money, but I've seen kids being bullied time and time again because they didn't have the right sneakers or their purse wasn't designer.

Although, after seeing the fees to attend this place, I'm not sure anyone will have money issues.

Dad promised me that this would be our last move and that he would ensure I had the best education to make up for it. It seems he was serious.

I lean closer to the mirror and inspect my neck—or rather, how good a job my concealer is doing.

The marks from that night might be fading now, but they're still more than visible.

By some miracle, I managed to sneak back into the house that night without anyone noticing my absence. I heard Dad's car pull into the driveway not thirty minutes later, and by the time he knocked on my door to check on me, I was freshly showered and pretending to be fast asleep. The reality was that I didn't manage to find any rest until long after the sun began to rise, my head full of images of the wicked boy in the graveyard.

If I was honest with myself, I didn't want to walk away.

There was obvious pain in his eyes. Hell, he was spending his evening sitting beside a headstone; it was clear he was dealing with something painful. I wanted to ask about it, to be a shoulder to cry on, or at least a nonjudgmental ear to listen to whatever he needed to get off his chest.

But the look in his eyes before I walked away told me he didn't want any of that, despite how much he clearly needed it.

I understand why he didn't want to tell me his name. It was never meant to be anything more than two broken souls colliding in the darkness. I never even meant to give him mine. It just fell from my lips after he demanded it. And I hate that it did, because now I know he can find me if he so desires. I'd rather be anonymous, like he is.

"Stella, are you ready?" my dad's voice booms up the stairs.

"Yeah, coming."

With one final look at myself in the mirror, I grab my cell and take a quick selfie to send to my friends on the other side of the pond before dropping it into my purse and heading out.

"You look—"

"Ridiculous?" I ask when I jump down the last two steps to join my dad in the hallway.

"No, you look beautiful."

"Is that what this fancy school requires?" I deadpan.

"Stella," he warns.

"I'm joking, Dad. I'm sure it's a fantastic school."

"I've got a surprise for you," he says, and it's only then I notice the smile he was trying to hide.

Butterflies erupt as I consider the only real thing it could be.

"It's in the driveway."

"Yesss," I hiss. "I love you, I love you," I chant, throwing myself into his embrace.

"I know things haven't been easy since we moved here."

Understatement of the century.

"But I promise that everything I'm doing is for you and your safety."

"It's London, Dad. Not Damascus."

"I know, sweetheart." His use of that name makes my entire body jolt as I remember it falling from someone else's lips. Thankfully, he doesn't notice my reaction. "I promise it will get better. I just needed to smooth a few things over with some associates."

"Riiight." I'm used to him being vague as fuck about what he actually does for a living, so I'm not exactly expecting a detailed reason as to why I've been stuck in this place for weeks on end. "It's fine, Dad. I get it." I mean, I don't, but I trust him, so I don't have much choice.

"I thought I could follow you in, make sure you get settled okay."

I narrow my eyes at him. He hasn't taken me to my first day at a new school since I was thirteen. I'm not sure why he feels the need to now.

"I'll be fine. This is just another day for me."

Regret passes through his features.

"I'm sorry—"

"Don't, Dad. Please. It's just another new school. I've got this."

He doesn't look happy about it, but he accepts it, and after dropping a kiss to my forehead, he stands aside.

"If you need me, call me. Calvin has his phone on him too," he says, referring to our head of security who moved over with us.

"Everything will be fine. I'm sure I can handle the elite teenagers of London."

"I'm sure you can, sweetheart. Have a good day. Angie is going to cook your favorite tonight."

"Great. I'm looking forward to it."

With a smile I don't really feel, I head for the front door.

That all changes when I get a look at what's waiting for me.

My new car.

The sleek lines of my new Porsche 911 brings a genuine smile to my lips and makes my muscles twitch to drop into the driver's seat and see what she's capable of.

She's matte black, just like the one I was forced to leave behind, but she's a newer model, and I can't wait to see the differences.

The purr of the engine and the incredibly soft red leather seats make the drive toward my new school almost enjoyable.

The parking lot is damn near full when I pull up, pointing to the fact that my extra-long detour here was probably just a little too long.

Unlike the school parking lots I'm used to, there are no rust-bucket cars. Instead, it's full of top of the line BMWs, Mercedes, Jaguars, and every other expensive makes and models I can think of—including a few Aston Martins and even a Bentley.

"Well, you're sure not in Kansas anymore, Doukas," I mutter to myself as I kill the engine and look out at the students all dressed the same as I am, loitering around and waiting for the day to start.

With my head held high, I climb from the car, throw my purse over my shoulder, and head for the main doors.

I came here with Dad the other week to get through all the paperwork for my enrollment and make a decision about the subjects I wanted to take, but the place was deserted then, the total opposite to what it is now.

I feel the stares of the other students as I make my way to reception, but I don't return their attention. I just focus on where I need to go. That is, until a tingle races down the left-hand side of my body, and I have no choice but to look to see what caused it.

I regret it instantly, because I immediately lock onto a pair of dark, angry eyes I'd recognize anywhere.

He stands from the bench he's sitting on top of and takes a step toward me, his increasing anger twisting his now clearly visible face. It's even more angular than I thought in the darkness.

He's gorgeous. Really fucking gorgeous.

Dropping my eyes lower, I take in his open collar and loose-hanging tie. He's not wearing his blazer and instead has his white shirt sleeves rolled up to his elbows, revealing strong, corded, inked forearms that I was unable to see in the graveyard before I get to his skinny pants that encase his long legs.

I really didn't stand a chance against him that night, did I?

It's not until he's right in front of me that I realize he didn't move alone, because there are four other guys flanking him.

"Is this her?" one of them asks in his smooth British accent.

"Yes," he drawls, his eyes eating me up. But I don't think it's to eat me like he did that night. His hunger is deadly right now in a way that sends a shiver of fear racing down my spine, and it takes a lot to make me react that way, so it's really saying something.

"You should run while you've got the chance, Hellion. You've just written your own death certificate, stepping foot in Knight's Ridge territory."

Stella and Sebastian's story will continue in Wicked Knight coming 21th October 2021
PRE-ORDER NOW

You can meet Stella before she moved to
London in Rosewood High.
Start the series with Thorn.
DOWNLOAD NOW

THORN
SNEAK PEEK

CHAPTER ONE
Amalie

"I think you'll really enjoy your time here," Principal Hartmann says. He tries to sound cheerful about it, but he's got sympathy oozing from his wrinkled, tired eyes.

This shouldn't have been part of my life. I should be in London starting university, yet here I am at the beginning of what apparently my junior year at an American high school I have no idea about aside from its name and the fact my mum attended many years ago. A lump climbs up my throat as thoughts of my parents hit me without warning.

"I know things are going to be different and you might feel that you're going backward, but I can assure you it's the right thing to do. It will give you the time you need to... adjust and to put some serious thought into what you want to do once you graduate."

Time to adjust. I'm not sure any amount of time will be enough to learn to live without my parents and being shipped across the Pacific to start a new life in America.

"I'm sure it'll be great." Plastering a fake smile on my face, I take the timetable from the principal's hand and stare down at it. The butterflies that were already fluttering around in my stomach erupt to the point I might just throw up over his chipped Formica desk.

Math, English lit, biology, gym, my hands tremble until I see something that instantly relaxes me, *art and film studies.* At least I got my own way with something.

"I've arranged for someone to show you around. Chelsea is the captain of the cheer squad, what she doesn't know about the school isn't worth knowing. If you need anything, Amalie, my door is always open."

Nodding at him, I rise from my chair just as a soft knock sounds out and a cheery brunette bounces into the room. My knowledge of American high schools comes courtesy of the hours of films I used to spend my evenings watching, and she fits the stereotype of captain to a tee.

"You wanted something, Mr. Hartmann?" she sings so sweetly it makes even my teeth shiver.

"Chelsea, this is Amalie. It's her first day starting junior year. I trust you'll be able to show her around. Here's a copy of her schedule."

"Consider it done, sir."

"I assured Amalie that she's in safe hands."

I want to say it's my imagination but when she turns her big chocolate eyes on me, the light in them diminishes a little.

"Lead the way." My voice is lacking any kind of enthusiasm and from the narrowing of her eyes, I don't think she misses it.

I follow her out of the room with a little less

bounce in my step. Once we're in the hallway, she turns her eyes on me. She's really quite pretty with thick brown hair, large eyes, and full lips. She's shorter than me, but then at five foot eight, you'll be hard pushed to find many other teenage girls who can look me in the eye.

Tilting her head so she can look at me, I fight my smile. "Let's make this quick. It's my first day of senior year and I've got shit to be doing."

Spinning on her heels, she takes off and I rush to catch up with her. "Cafeteria, library." She points then looks down at her copy of my timetable. "Looks like your locker is down there." She waves her hand down a hallway full of students who are all staring our way, before gesturing in the general direction of my different subjects.

"Okay, that should do it. Have a great day." Her smile is faker than mine's been all morning, which really is saying something. She goes to walk away, but at the last minute turns back to me. "Oh, I forgot. That over there." I follow her finger as she points to a large group of people outside the open double doors sitting around a bunch of tables. "That's *my* group. I should probably warn you now that you won't fit in there."

I hear her warning loud and clear, but it didn't really need saying. I've no intention of befriending the cheerleaders, that kind of thing's not really my scene. I'm much happier hiding behind my camera and slinking into the background.

Chelsea flounces off and I can't help my eyes from following her out toward *her* group. I can see from here that it consists of her squad and the football team. I can also see the longing in other student's eyes as they walk past them. They either want to be them or want to be part of their stupid little gang.

Jesus, this place is even more stereotypical than I was expecting.

Unfortunately, my first class of the day is in the direction Chelsea just went. I pull my bag up higher on my shoulder and hold the couple of books I have tighter to my chest as I walk out of the doors.

I've not taken two steps out of the building when my skin tingles with awareness. I tell myself to keep my head down. I've no interest in being their entertainment but my eyes defy me, and I find myself looking up as Chelsea points at me and laughs. I knew my sudden arrival in the town wasn't a secret. My mum's legacy is still strong, so when they heard the news, I'm sure it was hot gossip.

Heat spreads from my cheeks and down my neck. I go to look away when a pair of blue eyes catch my attention. While everyone else's look intrigued, like they've got a new pet to play with, his are haunted and angry. Our stare holds, his eyes narrow as if he's trying to warn me of something before he menacingly shakes his head.

Confused by his actions, I manage to rip my eyes from his and turn toward where I think I should be going.

I only manage three steps at the most before I crash into something—or somebody.

"Shit, I'm sorry. Are you okay?" a deep voice asks. When I look into the kind green eyes of the guy in front of me, I almost sigh with relief. I was starting to wonder if I'd find anyone who wasn't just going to glare at me. I know I'm the new girl but shit. They must experience new kids on a weekly basis, I can't be that unusual.

"I'm fine, thank you."

"You're the new British girl. Emily, right?"

"It's Amalie, and yeah... that's me."

"I'm so sorry about your parents. Mom said she was friends with yours." Tears burn my eyes. Today is hard enough without the constant reminder of everything I've lost. "Shit, I'm sorry. I shouldn't have—"

"It's fine," I lie.

"What's your first class?"

Handing over my timetable, he quickly runs his eyes over it. "English lit, I'm heading that way. Can I walk you?"

"Yes." His smile grows at my eagerness and for the first time today my returning one is almost sincere.

"I'm Shane, by the way." I look over and smile at him, thankfully the hallway is too noisy for us to continue any kind of conversation.

He seems like a sweet guy but my head's spinning and just the thought of trying to hold a serious conversation right now is exhausting.

Student's stares follow my every move. My

skin prickles as more and more notice me as I walk beside Shane. Some give me smiles but most just nod in my direction, pointing me out to their friends. Some are just downright rude and physically point at me like I'm some fucking zoo animal awoken from its slumber.

In reality, I'm just an eighteen-year-old girl who's starting somewhere new, and desperate to blend into the crowd. I know that with who I am—or more who my parents were—that it's not going to be all that easy, but I'd at least like a chance to try to be normal. Although I fear I might have lost that the day I lost my parents.

"This is you." Shane's voice breaks through my thoughts and when I drag my head up from avoiding everyone else around me, I see he's holding the door open.

Thankfully the classroom's only half full, but still, every single set of eyes turn to me.

Ignoring their attention, I keep my head down and find an empty desk toward the back of the room.

Once I'm settled, I risk looking up. My breath catches when I find Shane still standing in the doorway, forcing the students entering to squeeze past him. He nods his head. I know it's his way of asking if I'm okay. Forcing a smile onto my lips, I nod in return and after a few seconds, he turns to leave.

THORN and the rest of the ROSEWOOD series are now LIVE.

DOWNLOAD TO CONTINUE READING

ABOUT THE AUTHOR

Tracy Lorraine is a *USA Today* and *Wall Street Journal* bestselling new adult and contemporary romance author. Tracy has recently turned thirty and lives in a cute Cotswold village in England with her husband, baby girl and lovable but slightly crazy dog. Having always been a bookaholic with her head stuck in her Kindle, Tracy decided to try her hand at a story idea she dreamt up and hasn't looked back since.

Be the first to find out about new releases and offers. Sign up to my newsletter here.

If you want to know what I'm up to and see teasers and snippets of what I'm working on, then you need to be in my Facebook group. Join Tracy's Angels here.

Keep up to date with Tracy's books at

www.tracylorraine.com

ALSO BY TRACY LORRAINE

Avoiding Temptation #6

Chasing Temptation #7

Rebel Ink Series

Hate You #1

Trick You #2

Defy You #3

Play You #4

Inked (A Rebel Ink/Driven Crossover)

Rosewood High Series

Thorn #1

Paine #2

Savage #3

Fierce #4

Hunter #5

Faze (#6 Prequel)

Fury #6

Legend #7

Maddison Kings University Series

TMYM: Prequel

TRYS #1

TDYW #2

TBYS #3

TVYC #4

TDYD #5

TDYR #6

TRYD #7

Ruined Series

Ruined Plans #1

Ruined by Lies #2

Ruined Promises #3

Never Forget Series

Never Forget Him #1

Never Forget Us #2

Everywhere & Nowhere #3

Chasing Series

Chasing Logan

The Cocktail Girls

His Manhattan

Her Kensington

Printed in Dunstable, United Kingdom